MW00930046

S.T.I.N.K. & Co.

by Rosie McCormick
illustrated by Simon Paulson

Contents

PEARSON
Longman

Text © Rosie McCormick 2003
Series editors: Martin Coles and Christine Hall

PEARSON EDUCATION LIMITED
Edinburgh Gate
Harlow
Essex CM20 2JE
England

www.longman.co.uk

The right of Rosie McCormick to be identified as the author of this work has been asserted by her in accordance with the Copyright, Designs and Patents Act, 1988.

All rights reserved. No part of this publication may be reproduced, stored in a retrieval system, or transmitted in any form or by any means, electronic, mechanical, photocopying, recording, or otherwise without either the prior written permission of the Publishers or a licence permitting restricted copying in the United Kingdom issued by the Copyright Licensing Agency Ltd, 90 Tottenham Court Road, London W1P 9HE.

First published 2003
Third impression 2005
ISBN 0582 79616 4

Illustrated by Simon Paulson

Printed in China
WC/03

The publishers' policy is to use paper manufactured from sustainable forests.

The Initiation

Stevie flipped me over his back with a great deal of ease. It was as if he were throwing a handful of salt over his left shoulder to ward off bad luck. I landed in the school sandpit with an almighty thud and gasped as oxygen left my lungs in one big explosion of outgoing air. Gritty, wet sand rose up around my body and clung to my eyelids, nose and mouth. I struggled to breathe. But despite my discomfort, I did not complain. I was about to become a fully-fledged member of the Stevie Trovato Investigates Nasty Kids agency (otherwise known as S.T.I.N.K. & Co.) and I was, well almost, newly appointed Secret Agent Number 4. So, anything that happened to me from now on I had volunteered for.

I lifted myself up from the sandy mire like 'Swamp Thing' rising up from his marshy home and tried to draw breath. Stevie wasn't saying much, but I sensed that there was more to come. He had not *quite* finished welcoming me. I braced myself, silently clinging to my reasons for joining forces with a madman. Suddenly, and without warning, two figures emerged from behind the school's last remaining oak tree. They had obviously been positioned there, observing me, while Stevie played shot put with my body. I guessed that they were my fellow secret agents. Their identities, until now, known only to Stevie. From now on I would have to trust them implicitly. And for all I knew, I might even have to depend on them to save my life.

I stared up into their sullen, unfriendly faces and sighed. My comrades were none other than oddball dipstick Stumpy Hicks and the well-known raving loony Amy Martin. Both of whom were in Stevie's class. Stevie introduced us.

"Stumps, Amy, this is Owen O'Reilly. From now on you know him as Agent Number 4. Owen, Stumps is Agent Number 2 and Amy is Agent Number 3," said Stevie, sagely.

My fellow secret agents immediately proceeded to welcome me with a series of swift, forceful karate chops. They were testing my nerve, of course. As they moved their arms across my body like out-of-control marionettes, I just about managed to suppress an overwhelming inclination to cry out in agony and run for my life.

In fact, I don't think I even flinched. But my body couldn't help but notice that Amy, or rather Agent Number 3, was especially keen to prove that girls are as capable as boys when it comes to inflicting serious physical pain on other people. She certainly won me over to her side as far as that argument is concerned.

When the last blow had been struck, Amy and Stumps stood in front of me and bowed. Then in unison they screamed, *"S.T.I.N.K!"*

I, for my part, remained motionless; my mind focused on holding every muscle in my body perfectly still. I suspected that I resembled a startled rabbit and not a cool, unfathomable tough guy. But Stevie seemed satisfied that my initiation ceremony had gone well. He stood before me with his arms folded, his dark hair greased back, smiling the warm, affectionate smile of the benevolent Godfather-like leader he believed himself to be.

"And now that we've welcomed Agent Number 4, I suggest that we get down to business," he said, authoritatively. "Okay guys, I'll begin by going over the rules of S.T.I.N.K. & Co. one last time."

Stevie spoke as if he were addressing the United Nations or the House of Commons. He was clearly in control and our job was to listen and agree. My fellow agents and I stared obediently at Stevie and nodded our heads in acknowledgement of his leadership.

"The first thing to remember is that during agency hours all agents must speak with an American accent. *Capisce?*" continued Stevie.

Once again we nodded to communicate the fact that we understood rule number one.

"Second, when we're working on a case we all wear black. There are two reasons for this: one, black looks cool; two, it will help to identify

us as members of a successful organisation. Okay?"

The head nodding continued while I made a mental checklist of all the clothes I owned in the colour black. All I could think of were seven pairs of black socks.

"Now, if I were to ask you to sum up S.T.I.N.K. & Co. in a simple, three-word sentence, kind of like a mission statement, what would you say?" asked Stevie, while tipping his head to one side in eager anticipation of our answers.

Instead, we, his hand-picked agents, stood before our leader looking decidedly blank. I could see Stumpy moving his fingers against his leg, as if counting off the number of words he had in his head. 'We are lunatics' sounded good to me but I didn't volunteer to share my thoughts with my team. Amy did, however.

"We are kind of like gangsters," she offered, hopefully.

Stumpy's finger counting began again while Stevie looked visibly disappointed. This was clearly not the answer he had in mind.

"No, no, no! We are not like gangsters," Stevie exclaimed painfully. "Our job is to solve problems. We solve problems. That's what I was looking for. We troubleshoot. We investigate. We sort things out. If people come to us, we help them. For example, someone might say, 'Hey Stevie, that scumbag James keeps flushing my football kit down the toilet, can you have a word?' or 'Simon Hutton keeps putting gloop in my lunch box,

can you deal with him?' You see?" said Stevie. "Do you get where I'm coming from?"

"Oh yeah," said Amy. "I get it now. Cool!"

"Okay, let's move on," continued Stevie, clearly relieved that Agent Number 3 finally understood that we were not gangland sharks.

"Now as you know, we can't do this work for free," said Stevie, once again glancing sideways at us to make sure that we were nodding our heads in agreement. "No, that's right! We're running a business. Everything has its price, so the deal is we charge two bucks for something simple and four bucks for something more challenging. We split everything four ways. Agreed?" Stevie took off his school blazer, draped it across his shoulders and put a chunky crayon in his mouth by way of a pretend cigar.

I could see that the agency was a smart idea. A good way of making some extra cash. Two bucks (or pounds if you're a normal person) for something straightforward and four pounds for something more challenging were good rates of employment, even if it was all going to be split four ways. In fact, this was the very reason I had thrown caution to the wind and joined forces with someone as crazy as Stevie Trovato.

"Are there any questions?" Stevie asked, finally happy that he had covered all the relevant points.

There was *one* thing bothering me. Well, one

thing *really* bothering me, and this looked like it might be the best time to mention it. It was of course the agency's name. Although it certainly identified Stevie as its founder, I couldn't help worrying that it might cast a slight shadow, if not an enormous black cloud, upon our reputation. Well, *my* reputation to be precise.

"I have a question Agent Number 1," I said, nervously. "I was wondering if the name of the agency might give people the wrong idea. I mean, it's just a thought really, but do you think that people might be put off – just a little – by it?"

I had toned down what I really wanted to say – "Surely we can think of something even more ridiculous than S.T.I.N.K. & Co." – because Stevie's eyebrows had started to twitch as I spoke. Now they were moving up and down. I don't know about you, but experience has taught me that moving eyebrows usually means "Be careful what you say, it could be dangerous."

Stevie's eyebrows finally settled down. But he remained silent for several seconds. Then he removed the crayon from his mouth and breathed pretend cigar smoke in my face.

"If I thought the name was a problem, I'd

change it. But it's not a problem. It's an unforgettable name. It's unique and that makes it perfect. So don't worry about it," said Stevie ominously, as he patted my face and then pinched my cheek.

Well at least I was certain about one thing. Stevie was completely untouched by the burden of a sensitive nature. The agency's name did not embarrass him – in fact, he thought it was perfect. And as the others did not seem to share my reservations, I sighed and accepted my fate. I was now in the company of crazy people.

"Okay agents. We have an assignment that needs our urgent attention. Here's the problem," explained Stevie. "You know that brainy kid Nigel Bennett? Well, Shane Maxwell is making Nige do his homework for him. So braino has paid us four bucks to let Shane know that braino doesn't like doing anyone else's homework except his own. I've told Nige that he can trust the good name of S.T.I.N.K. & Co. and that we'll have his problem solved in less than twenty-four hours," said Stevie, confidently. "So guys, I want you to meet me at my house at 1900 hours, that's 7 o'clock, Stumps. Tonight we pay Shane Maxwell a little visit."

The Final Preparations

Less than four hours later, dressed in my brother's black tracksuit, I kicked at the scattered piles of rotting leaves as I walked towards Stevie's house. I was going there under the pretence of helping him with his science homework.

It was a dark, drizzly, early October evening. Street lights lit up the wet roads making them glisten and shine. The smell of burning wood hung comfortingly in the cool night air.

It was my favourite time of the year. It smelled special with promises of Hallowe'en, Guy Fawkes and evenings in front of the TV with mugs of hot chocolate and buttered toast.

I got the better of my troubled mind by turning my attention to Saturday's football game. The kick-off was at 3 o'clock and it was my debut game with the Amersham Wanderers – Under Twelves. The

question was, would I still be alive on Saturday?

Stevie lived on the same housing estate as I did – Priory Gardens. His house was just five minutes away from mine. I turned into his road and spotted his dad's ice cream van parked in the driveway. I walked the last fifty metres to his house forcing myself not to turn back. I lifted up the latch on his garden gate. The gate creaked as I pushed it open and slammed shut as I let it go. As I walked up the newly surfaced front path I stared up at the Trovatos' neat, semi-detached abode. Lights were on in every room in the front of the house. Slowly I reached up towards the door and reluctantly rang the bell.

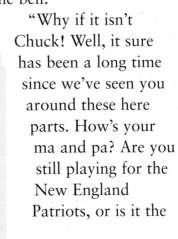

"Why if it isn't Chuck! Well, it sure has been a long time since we've seen you around these here parts. How's your ma and pa? Are you still playing for the New England Patriots, or is it the

Dallas Cowboys?" exclaimed Agent Number 3, as she held the front door open. She was wearing a black velvet party dress, sparkly black tights and black patent shoes. These were the first words she had ever spoken to me and I knew immediately why she was a member of S.T.I.N.K. & Co. She was completely and utterly mad.

It was apparent that Amy was taking Stevie's request that we speak with an American accent during agency hours quite seriously. But I sensed somehow that she had misunderstood his real intent.

"It's the Buckinghamshire Maniacs actually," I said, as I stepped passed her and went into Mr and Mrs Trovato's hall.

Immediately I heard Stevie's voice. "Up here dude," he called, from somewhere at the top of the stairs.

Agent Number 3 led the way. I watched her as she walked up the stairs in front of me. Her black, shiny tights had glittering stars running up the side of them. She had placed one hand on her hip and her dress made a swishing sound as it brushed against the staircase walls.

"We've been having trouble with the air-conditioning, but there's plenty of ice in the icebox," Amy said, turning her head to look at me as we reached the top of the stairs.

I did not reply. There was nothing I could say by way of a response. I was blatantly unskilled in the art of exchanging small talk with raving lunatics.

Stevie's bedroom was pretty much how I expected it to be. Pictures of his mostly American film idols stared out from every flat surface in the room. And piled in a corner were videotapes and DVDs of his favourite films. He also had a computer, a TV and a large black leather swivel chair.

Stevie welcomed me into his office, as he called it, with a friendly yet forceful slap across the back

of my head. Intuition told me not to return the greeting. Glancing at his attire, I had to admit he was looking pretty darn smart. He was wearing a black suit, white shirt and black tie. He also had on a black felt hat and sunglasses. Agent Number 2 was there too, dressed in his black football kit.

Agent Number 2 was a person of very few words. That's because he knew very few words. When he did speak, he sounded like some kind of bizarre, gurgling monster struggling to breathe. Stumpy was a sturdy, freckle-faced, brooding kind of a kid.

His role in all of this, as far as I could tell, was to act the part of the traditional silent heavy.

"Okay, dudes, now that you are all here I can tell you the plan. And let me tell you it's brilliant," said Stevie smiling broadly at us.

We waited in anxious silence as our leader savoured the moment. He was keenly aware of our nervous anticipation.

Then he continued. "We're going to sneak on board my dad's ice cream van just before he goes out on his round and we're going to deliver a message to Shane Maxwell: a message that he'll never forget!" announced Stevie.

I felt my entire body go completely numb as Stevie revealed to us that we were about to become stowaways on board his dad's ice cream van.

Slowly, as some feeling began to return to my body, I became aware that my legs had turned to jelly but my feet had become lead weights. I breathed deeply as my mind searched for a way out.

"Er, Stevie, don't you think that your dad might notice us sitting in the back of his van?" I asked, trying to stop my voice from shaking.

"No, dude," said Stevie confidently. "Two of you will hide behind some boxes of cones my dad's got stacked in the back; Stumpy will hide in one of the freezers and I will hide next to the other freezer!"

"Coool," screeched Stumpy, unaware of the obvious humour in that response.

"Now, just before you got here," said Stevie, referring to me, "Agent Number 2 recorded a little message for our pal Shane. We're gonna play it on the van's megaphone system when we get to Shane's house."

I sat down on Stevie's bed and took a few more deep breaths. "You're using Stumpy's voice ... I mean Agent Number 2. Is that a good idea? I mean ..."

"It sounds awesome, man. You won't believe how *great* it sounds," continued Stevie, ignoring me and pressing the play button on his tape deck.

The sound of Stumpy's voice filled the room and a cold chill ran down my spine as we listened to Stumpy's low, gravelly voice. When the message had played Stevie switched off the tape. There was an obvious glint in his eye. "Well man, what do you think? Pretty cool, huh?" he asked, not really looking for an answer.

"One thing's for sure, it will scare Shane, and perhaps a few other people as well. Like maybe even the entire neighbourhood," I offered by way of a response.

"Ace," said Stevie looking hopeful.

"So how do we get the tape onto your dad's megaphone system?" I asked, hoping that this might be the key part of the plan that Stevie had overlooked.

"Easy. My dad will be stopping at Uncle Ronaldo's house tonight to pick up some lemon and lime ice pops. While he's in the house I'll sneak into the front of the van and switch 'Greensleeves' for Stumpy's track. Then, and this is the icing on the cake, my dad always

starts his round by parking opposite Shane's house on Orchard Road. It's like I said. *Brilliant.*

"Oh, and one final thing, while my dad is parked opposite Shane's house wondering what's happened to his ice cream music, we're going to get out of the van and hold up a gigantic glow-in-the-dark banner that Agent Number 3 has made. Shane will know for sure that we are onto him. I figured we could all walk home from there without my dad knowing a thing."

There was nothing more I could say. It was clear that Stevie had worked out every detail of his 'brilliant' plan. He was even going to tell his mum that we were all going round to Stumpy's house to help him with his homework. I sat in silence on Stevie's bed waiting for further instructions.

"Okay, it's time to move. You three go and wait in the front garden while I get the keys and open up the back of the van. As soon as the doors are open, jump in while I put the keys back on the hall table," said Stevie finally.

And with that we all stood up and got ready to go.

The Ice Cream Van Stowaways

The rain fell in large drops as we stood in the front garden waiting to board the Trovato ice cream van. Keen to protect her party dress from the downpour, Amy opened her fluorescent pink umbrella with its Statue of Liberty motif.

"I'll have a cherry cola and a peanut butter and jelly sandwich please. And make it snappy. Gee, the elevator is taking forever to arrive. If it isn't here in two seconds I'm gonna kick someone's butt," she said, while moving her umbrella towards us in an attempt to shield us from the rain. Both Stumpy and I shuffled to one side, refusing to stand under it.

After a minute or two, Stevie stepped out of his house. We watched him as he sauntered towards the van. It was as if he were going out for a drive in his car on a Sunday afternoon. We waited anxiously as he opened up the back of the van.

Then seconds later we all piled in.

It was just as Stevie had said. There were several boxes of cones and wafers stacked on one side of the van and there were two large freezers. We waited for Stevie to return before taking up our positions.

"Agents 3 and 4, you sit behind those boxes of cones. Stumps you climb into this freezer. You'll be sorry to hear it's not switched on," said Stevie, as he reappeared at the back of the van and began to climb in. "My dad only uses it in the summer when he's really busy."

I have to say Stumpy did look visibly disappointed.

"I'll hide in the corner next to the other freezer," said Stevie finally.

Moments later we heard the sound of Mr

Trovato whistling and humming to himself as he
opened up the front of the van and climbed into
the driver's seat.

Mr Trovato was one of those ice cream sellers
who sold ice cream from his van all year round.
Even in the middle of winter he could be seen
selling frozen treats dressed only in a white T-shirt
and beige cotton trousers. If I moved my head
slightly to one side I could just about see the back

of his head
from my
position
behind the
box of
cones. I
watched him
as he started
up the engine,
adjusted a
slick of dark
hair in the
rear view
mirror, and
reversed the
ice cream van
out of the
driveway.

For the next four or five minutes we listened to the sound of Stevie's dad humming as we drove to Uncle Ronaldo's house. Then, when the van stopped suddenly, we knew that we had arrived at our first stop.

Stevie's dad didn't bother to turn off the engine. He just jumped out of the van and hurried towards a small, yellow-painted terraced house. He obviously didn't intend to be gone for long. Glancing up, I spotted an Italian flag flying from a flagpole at the top of the yellow house between the upstairs bedroom windows.

As soon as Stevie was satisfied that his dad was safely inside his uncle's house, he slid open the glass partition windows that separated the front of the van from the back and climbed across into the driver's seat. Then, quick as a flash, he switched the tapes.

While Stevie was doing this Amy and I stood up to stretch our legs and Stumpy popped his head up from inside the freezer.

After a few seconds, I glanced across at Stevie again. He was still sitting in the driver's seat, only now he was playing with the lights and the indicators.

It was then that I spotted a clearly horror-stricken man dressed in a blue raincoat standing a few metres away from the front of the van. He was staring at Stevie. After a few seconds he walked briskly towards the sliding glass service window at the side of the van and peered in.

Our eyes met. Next he spotted Amy. Finally, his eyes came to rest upon Stumpy who was still crouched in the freezer with his head popping out.

Although I couldn't see the man's face clearly in the darkness, I couldn't help thinking that he looked strangely familiar. My mind began to whirl as his angry, beady eyes glared at us. My entire life flashed before me as seconds later I suddenly realised who he was. He was none other than our headteacher, Mr Thorn.

Without hesitating, Mr Thorn banged on the glass service window and shouted, "What on earth are you all doing?"

Right on cue and with a grand flourish Amy stepped forward and opened up the service window. "Now what'll it be, honey?" she said in her best Texan accent. "We have sweet potato pie, blueberry pie, Grandma's home-made apple pie, and of course we have Mississippi mud pie."

Mr Thorn's face visibly paled and the corners of his mouth began to twitch nervously. I could see the whites of his eyes quite clearly. It was as if

a troop of grotesque, slime-slinging aliens had landed on Earth and had chosen him to be the first human to have contact with them. He appeared uncharacteristically lost for words. Speechless, in fact.

When he did recover his senses he marched away from us, round the front of the van to the driver's door. Seconds later the driver's door shot open and Mr Thorn's pointy head appeared inside the van. "Move over," he yelled at Stevie.

Stevie, startled by Mr Thorn's sudden appearance, did just as he was told.

Without further ado, Mr Thorn jumped in, clicked on a seat belt, adjusted the rear view mirror, slipped the van into first gear, released the hand brake and took off.

It was only then that it dawned on me that Mr Thorn was under the impression that we had stolen Mr Trovato's ice cream van. He had obviously jumped to the conclusion that Stevie had been driving it.

Mr Trovato appeared in his brother's doorway just in time to see his van being driven away by a man in a blue raincoat.

"Hey, what are you doing?" said Stevie, who had finally found his voice. "And slow down, we'll get done for speeding."

"Be quiet. Just be grateful that I spotted you bunch of idiots," yelled Mr Thorn. "Who knows what could have happened?" he shouted, almost spitting the words at Stevie.

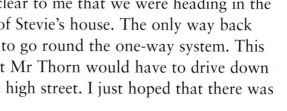

Stevie looked puzzled but remained silent. Amy and Stumpy appeared not to have noticed the sudden change of plan.

It was clear to me that we were heading in the direction of Stevie's house. The only way back there was to go round the one-way system. This meant that Mr Thorn would have to drive down the village high street. I just hoped that there was no one around who might recognise us.

"My dad's not going to like this one bit," braved Stevie, as the familiar high street shops whizzed by.

Mr Thorn chose to ignore Stevie as he changed up into fifth gear.

I stared out of the window while contemplating my fate. The fact is, I had never in my wildest dreams imagined that I would one day be hurtling through the night in the back of a stolen ice cream van, which was being driven at a dangerously high speed by my headteacher. Life sure is strange.

Eventually the silence was once again broken by Amy and her North American rantings. "I just lurve pistachio ice cream," she said to no one in particular. "Boys, when I get a car it will be a Cadillac, or maybe a Buick, or perhaps a Mustang! I'll just drive and drive with the wind blowing in my hair. I'll go south to Texas. Or maybe I'll go west to California. I'll stop at diners and eat grits and hash browns. It'll be just swell!"

She was clearly inspired by Mr Thorn's driving but I had had enough. "Planet Earth calling Amy," I said. "Listen, for your information, when Stevie asked us to speak with American accents he didn't mean that we were no longer compelled to communicate with our fellow human beings. So what the heck are you talking about? Do you even know?"

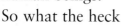

Amy didn't answer. Instead she gave me a look that promised punishment at a later date and then brushed past me to stand next to Stumpy who was still sitting in the freezer.

I'd had enough of S.T.I.N.K. & Co. to last me a lifetime. And I had come to a terrible conclusion. I was obviously more insane than my fellow agents, because I had imagined myself to *be* sane. It was a defining moment for me and it was clear that I had to rethink my life and future plans.

Mr Thorn continued to drive really fast. All we needed now was to be stopped by the police. Because he was driving so fast he missed the right turn on the roundabout that led to Priory Gardens – twice. And so twice we hurtled round the roundabout. Having made the turn he then proceeded to stall the van. We had come to a halt on a leafy, residential road.

It was Stevie who noticed that we had stalled right outside Shane Maxwell's house. Quick as a flash and not one to miss an opportunity, he leaned forward and pressed the 'PLAY' button on the tape deck. Then he calmly sat back in his seat as if he was about to listen to his favourite band.

37

Seconds later Stumpy's voice hit the airwaves. Mr Thorn suddenly stopped turning the key in the ignition as the demonic sound of Stumpy Hicks' voice rose up into the crisp, night air.

"Thisss izzz a messsaaage forrr Shaaane Maaaxwell. S.T.I.N.K. & Co. arrre orrrderrriiing youuu tooo dooo yerrr owwwn hooomeworrrk orrr elllssse S.T.I.N.K. & Co. willl cooome loookiiing fooorrrr yeerrrr. Yeeerrrr noothiing but a liiitle scuuumm buuucket!"

As I watched Mr Thorn's stunned reaction, I couldn't help feeling sorry for him. It was clear that he didn't have a clue what was going on. He must have felt like he had stumbled into someone else's bad dream. I know I did.

As the message played for the second time Stevie turned round, smiled at us and gave us the thumbs up. I didn't realise it but this was the signal to display the glow-in-the-dark banner that Stumpy had been sitting on in the freezer.

Without hesitating Stumpy whipped it out from underneath him, opened up the service window and then he and Amy waved the banner in the general direction of Shane's house. It read:

SHANE MAXWELL!! NB SAYS GET YOUR OWN BRAIN!

Having completed their banner waving, Stumps and Amy moved back inside the van just in time for me to see Shane, his baby sister and his mum and dad peering anxiously out through the living room window.

I'm pretty sure the Maxwells recognised Mr Thorn. What they were thinking I can only imagine. Perhaps they thought that this bizarre spectacle had been specially organised by the Head in order to demonstrate a new and unique approach to school discipline.

For his part I could tell that Mr Thorn was considering whether an explanation would be timely or whether he should simply opt for a speedy getaway. As he finally got the engine going, he chose option number two and we shot off like a rocket.

"Turn it off, *now!*" Mr Thorn roared at Stevie, as we sped to the end of Shane's road. He was of course referring to S.T.I.N.K. & Co.'s special message to Shane, which was still being broadcast.

At this point I couldn't help feeling a tad smug. I had predicted that one way or another our neighbourhood would hear Stumpy's voice – and tremble.

Stevie leaned forward and replaced Stumpy's tape with his dad's. Then once again he turned

round and smiled at us. Amy returned the smile, all the while batting her long eyelashes at him, while Stumpy grunted and raised a clenched fist in the air. Me, I just wanted to scream "Get me out of here." But who was there to listen to my cry for help?

Eventually Mr Thorn turned into Stevie's road at high speed with 'Greensleeves' blaring loudly from the Trovato ice cream van. By this time I had reached the conclusion that Mr Thorn had once harboured ambitions to be a Formula One racing driver. What he could

do with an ice cream van was incredible. I could only imagine what he could have done on a race track in a real car.

We came to a screeching halt outside Stevie's house. Needless to say our noisy intrusion into the silent and peaceful road didn't go unnoticed.

Members of the Neighbourhood Watch promptly sprang into action. Doors opened, curtains were pulled back and men wearing knitted cardigans and carrying torches appeared as if from nowhere.

Mr Thorn ordered Stevie to get out while he walked to the back of the van and banged on the doors. "OUT, NOW!" he yelled, at the top of his voice, seemingly unaware of the commotion he was causing. And so we stepped out.

I've never before seen a more astonished looking bunch of people in all my life. Mrs Trovato was by this time standing completely motionless in her front garden with a startled expression on her face, while various neighbours were standing in open doorways looking extremely puzzled and bewildered.

Mr Thorn pointed firmly towards the Trovatos' house. We obeyed his command by shuffling silently towards Stevie's open front door. Actually Agents 2, 3 and 4 shuffled. Agent Number 1 strolled and whistled as if he didn't have a care in the world. Me, I held my head down low – not because I thought I had done something terribly wrong but because I was more embarrassed than I had ever been in my entire life.

Mission Accomplished

Mrs Trovato was clearly unsure of how to react. No doubt she was wondering where her husband had disappeared to, what we were all doing in the ice cream van, and how come Mr Thorn had gained possession of the vehicle that earned the Trovato family a healthy income. That's more than enough confusion for anyone.

It was clear to me that at some point soon one of us was going to have to reveal to Mr Thorn the fact that he had actually stolen the ice cream van from Stevie's dad. While we all stood in the Trovato hallway, I wondered which one of us was going to find the courage to tell him.

As Mrs Trovato shut the front door, Mr Thorn turned to her and said with great confidence, "Don't worry, Mrs Trovato, I've got everything under control. But I must say that it was fortunate for all concerned that I spotted them in time!"

His tone, not to mention his choice of words, implied that Mrs Trovato should be grateful to him. And so she expressed her heart-felt gratitude.

"Thaaank you Meeester Thorn. Thaaank you so very much," said Mrs Trovato in her best Italian–English accent. "Oh tank God for Mr Thorn!"

I wasn't so sure that Mr Trovato was going to be quite so grateful. We would have to wait and see.

"Now, if you don't mind I would like to phone these children's parents. Can I use your phone?" Mr Thorn asked.

"Yes, please do!" replied Mrs Trovato.

Mr Thorn's beady eyes once again met mine. He stared ominously at me even though he was speaking to all four of us.

"I want you to write down your telephone numbers on this piece of paper," said Mr Thorn, as he reached for the notepad and pen on the hall table.

"Then I want you all to go and sit in Mrs Trovato's living room," he continued.

"Is that okay with you, Mrs Trovato?" he asked again.

"Please. Yes. Perhaps they like a little cake an' a juice," she replied.

"I don't think they deserve treats at the moment," replied a stern Mr Thorn. "I will explain the entire situation to you as soon as I have phoned their parents."

Mrs Trovato looked perplexed as Amy, Stumpy and I stepped up to write down our telephone numbers on the pad. When Stumpy finally remembered his phone number we were ushered into Stevie's front room along with Mrs Trovato.

We sat there in silence for a while until eventually Stevie spoke.

"Mum, Mr Thorn's just nicked Dad's ice cream van," he said, as cool as you like. "Dad's gonna go mad!"

"No, no. Some mistake I sure," replied Mrs Trovato. "In any case, 'ow you know dis? Why you no 'elp Stumpy with is 'omework?"

She was beginning to get the picture, I could tell. She was finally beginning to wonder whether we'd actually been at Stumpy's house at all.

"And you," Mrs Trovato said, looking at Amy. "What you do with these naughty boys? You such a good girl," she said earnestly.

It would have been best for everyone if she had simply ignored Amy, but she hadn't. Amy replied by smiling at Mrs Trovato. Seconds later she stood up and walked into the centre of the room.

"The weather report says there's a twister heading this way. We'd better ride out and check that the cattle are okay. You know there are coyotes in them there hills!"

said Amy as if she were providing us with some crucial information.

Mrs Trovato looked dazed. "What she say, Stevie?" she asked. "I no understand."

But Stevie didn't get a chance to reply because at that very moment Mrs Trovato spotted Mr Trovato getting out of a taxi just in front of the house.

"Goodness, what is 'appening?" exclaimed Mrs Trovato as she rushed out of the living room to open up the front door. We were all right behind her. We didn't want to miss Mr Trovato as he confronted the blue-raincoated thief.

Mr Thorn had just put the phone down, having summoned his final parent to the Trovato home, when an angry Mr Trovato appeared in the

hallway. At first he didn't seem to notice Mr
Thorn. He was completely flustered and he
was muttering something about a moron, an
idiot, and a thief. Oh and I do believe he
mentioned the word 'murder' before uttering
several Italian curses.

Mrs Trovato tried to calm him down by telling
him not to worry. "Don't worry, Angelo. Mr
Thorn has everything in control. You see 'ee is 'ere
to 'elp. I get you a coffee and some cake," she
said soothingly.

It was then that Mr Trovato spotted the cause
of his troubles. "What you doin' in my 'ouse?"
Mr Trovato yelled at Mr Thorn. "You stole my
ice cream van. I call the police. You crazy man!"

   And with that Mr Trovato picked up the
phone and began to dial 999. Fortunately for Mr
Thorn, Mrs Trovato overheard her husband's
angry words and rushed back into the hallway
just in time. She handed me a plate laden with
home-made chocolate cake before grabbing the
phone out of her husband's hands. "No, no,
Angelo. You make a mistake," she said, cutting
off the call.

"No Mum, he hasn't. Mr Thorn really did steal Dad's van," volunteered Stevie, clearly hoping to get our headteacher arrested.

"Yeah," chirped Amy, in support of Stevie. "He was on Highway 64 when the cops told him to pull over. He didn't listen, so they blew his tyres out. The van's a wreck!"

Amy always managed to render people speechless. Mr Trovato didn't say anything, but he did hastily open up the front door just to double-check that his tyres hadn't been shot to ribbons. Seconds later, and breathing a visible sigh of relief, he closed the door again having reassured himself that his ice cream van was still in one piece.

"Now, now, let's all calm down. I think I can explain," said a much less confident Mr Thorn.

"I was on my way home, walking along Orchard Road, when I spotted Stevie driving *your* ice cream van."

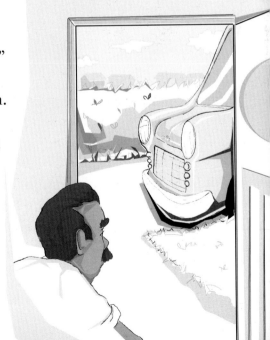

"Well, he wasn't actually driving it at the time. But he was sitting in the driver's seat. He had just indicated that he was about to pull out and he had put the headlights on."

"Fortunately, I was able to apprehend him just in time. The logical thing for me to do was to bring him and the van back here. Oh, and that's not all, these three were in the back of the van as well!" concluded Mr Thorn.

Mr Trovato remained silent for several moments while Mrs Trovato sat down on a chair in the hall. Her rosy cheeks had paled a little and she was looking quite bewildered.

Finally, an agitated Mr Trovato spoke. "Is impossible. I drove the van to Orchard Road. I park outside my brother's 'ouse. I go inside for few seconds to get icy pops.

"Then I come outside to see you driving my ice cream van down the road! Dat is what 'appened!"

"Well, I can assure you that Stevie and the

other three were in the van, otherwise why would
I have brought them all back here? I think we
need some answers, Mr Trovato, don't you?" said
a now very irate Mr Thorn.

Both men turned to look at us. They were
getting angry now. It was clear that we were
running out of time. Someone had to come up
with a reasonable explanation and fast. I looked
at Stevie. As Agent Number 1, I felt that it was
his responsibility to speak on our behalf. He
didn't look like he was going to say anything. But
Amy did.

"We say nothing without a lawyer. We know
our rights. Ain't that so, boys? And in any case,
we was hanging out on 14th and Broadway
when it happened. You ain't got nothin' on us."
As Amy spoke she placed a hand on her hip
and smiled defiantly at Mr Trovato and Mr
Thorn.

"Well that was helpful," I thought to myself.
"That's bound to get us off the hook."

Suddenly Mr Trovato grabbed Stevie by his
jacket collar and glared straight at him. "What
is going on? You tell me now Stevie, or you in
big trouble," screeched Mr Trovato. As he spoke
the end of his nose was just about touching
Stevie's.

"Okay, Dad, I'll tell you. But you're going to be sorry that you got so mad when you hear what really happened. You see, the truth is that all of us want to own ice cream vans when we grow up. We want to do what you do. And, as you are the best, I promised the guys – that includes Amy – that I would let them see you in action."

"So, yes, we did sneak on board the van. But we did it because we thought that was the best way to watch you but not disturb you while you were working," said Stevie without even blinking. "Isn't that right, guys?"

My fellow agents and I nodded our heads obediently and enthusiastically in the hope that Stevie's explanation had saved the day.

"I wasn't driving the van, Dad, I promise. I did sit in the driver's seat while you were in Uncle Ronaldo's house. But that was all. It was then that Mr Thorn came along and stole, I mean, took the van," concluded Stevie.

Slowly Mr Trovato let go of his son's collar. For several seconds he stared at Stevie. I could tell that he wanted to believe that this was the truth. Mr Thorn, on the other hand, looked decidedly unconvinced.

"Why you no talk to me about dis, Stevie? Why you no ask me? I thought you want to be a firefighter anyway," said Mr Trovato. His voice not *quite* as angry any more.

"No, I want to be just like you, Dad," said Stevie, warming to the part of proud and faithful son.

Mr Trovato ruffled his son's hair. He was clearly impressed by Stevie's devotion. Then he turned to us and smiled. "So you want to be like me, huh?" he asked. "When you are older I teach you. But no more sneaking in my van. Okay?"

"Okay!" Stumpy, Amy and I said in unison, while Stevie beamed and then winked at us. Then Mrs Trovato stood up and smiled at us lovingly. It was as if we had suddenly become part of her family.

"I knew there was good reason why dis 'appen. Tank God we sort it all out," she said, before disappearing into the kitchen to organise refreshments for her newly extended family and our parents who would no doubt be arriving soon.

It was Mr Thorn who decided to interrupt this moving scene of hero worship and bring us all back to reality.

"Well, perhaps it's best that we let the matter drop. But I would like to think that you have all learned a lesson tonight. I do not expect a repeat performance," he said, in a surprisingly calm voice. "And I apologise for any inconvenience I may have caused you, Mr Trovato. But you can see why I, shall we say, *misinterpreted* the situation. As for you, Owen, it comes as a great surprise to hear that you want to own an ice cream van one day. I was under the impression that you wanted to be a doctor like your grandfather."

I could not look Mr Thorn in the eye. Instead I stared down at my black trainers. It was obvious that he knew that I knew that Stevie had concocted one heck of a tall tale. But for some reason he had chosen not to shatter Mr Trovato's illusions about his son, or indeed about us.

"If you don't mind, I will wait to talk to the other children's parents, especially as I was the one who requested that they come here to collect them," he said finally.

"No problem Mr Thorn," said Mr Trovato. "Come through to kitchen and 'ave some coffee. Stevie, you take your friends to other room and watch TV. We bring you something nice as well."

We nodded our heads by way of acknowledging that this sounded like a good idea and shuffled behind Stevie as he made his way into the living room. As soon as we were safely behind closed doors Stevie turned to us and smiled. "Apart from a minor setback I think our first assignment went well, don't you?" he said, quite sincerely.

The minor setback was of course Mr Thorn.

"Ace," mumbled Stumpy.

"Piece of cake," said Amy.

I remained silent. I wasn't sure that I could put my thoughts into words. Not words that made sense anyway.

"What do you think, Agent Number 4? Mission accomplished or what?" asked Stevie, placing an arm around my shoulders.

"Well, we're still alive, it looks like we've avoided expulsion from school and we're not

going to be sent to a young offenders' detention centre. So yes, you could say that things have gone quite well!" I uttered miserably.

"Exactly. Just stick with me, kid. We're on our way to the big time!" said Stevie with great enthusiasm. "Now, I've been thinking about the power of advertising. I have a suggestion to make. I say we put ten per cent of our first month's earnings back into the business so that we can buy T-shirts with the agency's name printed on them. What do you think?"

I have to confess that I was speechless. Not only was Stevie completely untroubled by the events that had just unfolded, he was now suggesting that we appear in public wearing T-shirts with the letters S.T.I.N.K. & Co. emblazoned upon them. By way of concluding this shared moment, he slapped me across the back of the head as if to say, "Now what do you think of that for another brilliant plan?"

Fortunately my parents arrived just in time to save me from attempting to tell him that under no circumstances was I going to be seen in public wearing a T-shirt with S.T.I.N.K. & Co. written on it. (Even if Stumpy and Amy were ecstatic about the prospect.) Instead, I waited anxiously to be summoned into the hall and then bundled into the back of my dad's car.

For several minutes I sat and listened to the sound of mumbling in the hallway. I tried to hear exactly what Mr Thorn was saying to my parents, but he was speaking in deliberately hushed tones. No doubt he was conveying to them one of the most astonishing revelations of the evening: that I, his A-grade student, intended to join the Trovato ice cream empire rather than go to university and become a doctor. Just how my mum was going to take this I wasn't quite sure.

Eventually my dad popped his head into the living room, just as Mrs Trovato was serving up double helpings of chocolate cake and squash. I could tell from the expression on his face that there was no point asking him if I could stay a little longer.

I got up from my seat beside the piano and walked solemnly towards the door.

Stevie watched me go. "See you soon, dude," he said, almost affectionately.

"Yeah, see you soon, Stevie," I half-whispered, while my dad glared at me.

Seconds later, as my dad closed the Trovatos' front door behind us, I spotted Stevie, Amy and Stumpy peering out from behind Mrs Trovato's living room window. Incredibly, Stumpy held a clenched fist in the air, while Amy's hand was raised in a wave. Stevie was giving me the 'thumbs up' sign. It was a sincere gesture of solidarity by my fellow agents, and I have to confess that it did make me smile.

I was just about to wave back when my dad spotted them, too. Without hesitating he shoved

me into the back of our car and told me not to move, not to say anything and only to breathe if I really had to. Moments later, two cars pulled up just in front of ours and four concerned-looking parents suddenly appeared on the pavement outside the Trovatos' house. I had no doubt about who they were. Neither had Stumpy or Amy, for they were no longer standing at the window saluting me. But Stevie was still there, smiling broadly. He stood there smiling until our car disappeared into the chill, misty darkness of the night.

Upon Reflection

Two days had passed before Stevie, Amy, Stumpy and I had a chance to catch up with each other at school. I had been busy with the after-school science and chess clubs, while my fellow agents had detentions for not doing their homework. Not to mention the fact that my parents had banned me from hanging out with them again – ever!

But on Thursday, right after school, Stevie called an agency meeting at the sandpit in the field behind the computer room. When Thursday afternoon came round I found myself alarmingly eager to get to the assigned meeting place. I hated to admit it but I was kind of missing them.

I was, predictably, the last agent to arrive. Stevie, Amy and Stumpy were already there, standing on the edge of the sandpit laughing. Struggling to carry my too-heavy book bag, I lumbered towards them.

Stevie spotted me first. "Heh, Agent Number 4! Glad you could make it. How have you been, man?" he asked, enthusiastically.

"Okay, I guess," I said.

"Great," said Stevie. "I was just telling Agents 2 and 3 a joke. It's really funny," he said laughing out loud. "Listen to this! 'Doctor, Doctor, I think I need glasses,' said the boy. 'You've got that right, this is a video shop,' said the man."

Agents 1, 2 and 3 collapsed in fits of raucous laughter. It was a slightly funny joke I thought, but not hilarious. Nevertheless I did my best to join in.

Eventually, once we had regained our composure, Stevie decided that it was time to get down to business. In a more formal voice he announced that our meeting was now in session and that he had some important information for us.

"I've got good news, guys," he said. "Our first client, Nigel Bennett,

was so pleased with our work the other night that he not only paid us our fee but he gave us a tip as well. We earned ourselves five bucks this week. It seems that Shane Maxwell has stopped bothering old Nige. In fact, Shane is too afraid to even talk to him any more," said Stevie, looking as proud as punch. "Nige is going to pass the word around that ST.I.N.K. & Co. really do get the job done," he said, sincerely.

That news didn't surprise me one bit, I have to say. In fact it wouldn't surprise me if Shane Maxwell was too frightened to talk to anyone for quite some time.

"So, as agreed, we're going to split our earnings four ways," continued Stevie, decisively. "Right?"

"Right," Amy, Stumpy and I retorted.

I knew immediately that my fellow agents expected me to figure out the maths. They could tell that five divided by four doesn't work out evenly. But as to the correct answer, they were not too sure. "That makes one pound twenty-five pence each," I volunteered.

"That's right. One pound twenty-five," repeated Stevie. "Does anyone have any change?" he asked, anxiously.

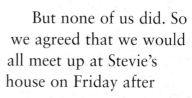

But none of us did. So we agreed that we would all meet up at Stevie's house on Friday after school to divide up our hard-earned cash – and to figure out what ten per cent of five pounds was so that we could start to save up for our S.T.I.N.K. & Co. T-shirts. (I'm ashamed to admit it, but the idea was beginning to grow on me.)

Then, after appointing me Treasurer of S.T.I.N.K. & Co. because I could add up, subtract and divide with some degree of accuracy, and with some stirring words about his hopes and dreams for the agency's future, Stevie dismissed us.

"Be cool!" he said, as he turned to walk away. "Be right and don't fight!"

I watched him as he walked off towards the school gate. With those wise words ringing in my ears I made my way home in the drizzle and grey of the late afternoon.

Hours later, as I lay in my bed watching the hazy, silver light of the moon cast shadows in my room, I became aware once again of that strange,

butterfly feeling in the pit of my stomach. I knew it was warning me to stay clear of the crazy world that Stevie Trovato inhabits. But I also knew that it was too late. I was feeling more than a little pleased that I had joined forces with someone as mad as Stevie. In fact, I was *even* beginning to like Stumpy and Amy. You see, I'd come to the conclusion that the world is a much more interesting place with people like them in it. They make life fun. And that's pretty cool – don't you think?